ADVENTURES IN COLONIAL AMERICA

ADVENTURES IN COLONIAL AMERICA

THE WINTER AT VALLEY FORGE

Survival and Victory

by James E. Knight

Illustrated by George Guzzi

Troll Associates

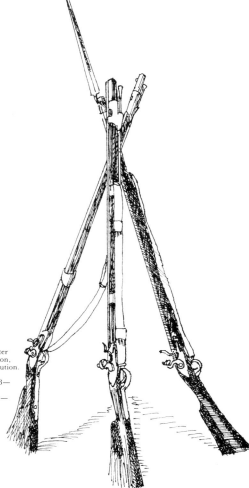

Library of Congress Cataloging in Publication Data

Knight, James E.
    The winter at Valley Forge.

    Summary: A soldier chronicles the harsh winter
colonial soldiers, led by General George Washington,
spend at Valley Forge during the American Revolution.
        1. Valley Forge (Pa.)—Juvenile literature.
2. United States—History—Revolution, 1775-1783—
Campaigns and battles—Juvenile literature.
[1. Valley Forge (Pa.) 2. United States—History—
Revolution, 1775-1783—Campaigns and battles]
I. Guzzi, George, ill. II. Title.
E234.K58   973.3 '341   81-23151
ISBN 0-89375-738-1   AACR2
ISBN 0-89375-739-X (pbk.)

THE WINTER AT VALLEY FORGE

Survival and Victory

Troll Associates

The wind is cold and piercing here at Valley Forge. We are about twenty miles northwest of Philadelphia—which fell to the enemy in September. This is a bleak and lonely place, but we must make preparations to stay here for some months, I fear.

Since our defeat by the British at Germantown in October, our situation has become steadily worse. Some days ago, we crossed the Schuylkill River into Gulph Mills on a temporary bridge made of covered wagons. We hoped to put a safe distance between ourselves and General Howe's troops, and yet remain close to the city. We must keep the enemy from advancing. I pray that by springtime, we will have regained enough strength to take back Philadelphia.

Early yesterday we left Gulph Mills for our winter quarters here at Valley Forge. The march was a difficult one, and I do not think that I, Corporal Toby Grimes, could have endured another moment of that journey.

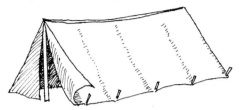

Marquee for Colonels

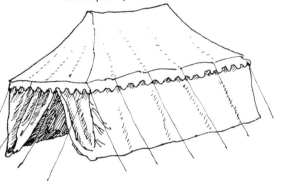

Wall Tent for Six Soldiers

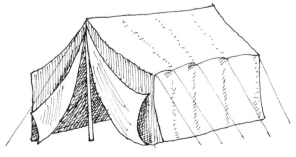

When we arrived in the evening, we fell immediately upon the ground, covering ourselves as best we could. Few had the energy to put up tent or shelter.

For some weeks, this army has awaited the arrival of provisions. We need both food and clothing. It is difficult to tell which is worse—hunger or the freezing weather. My men are dressed in rags, and only a few are lucky enough to have shoes. Even the officers are dressed poorly. General Washington rides among us, his stern, sad face showing his concern for his soldiers.

No one knows why the British have not pursued us across the river. Certainly they have the strength and numbers. But General Howe remains in Philadelphia. Perhaps he thinks we are beaten. If so, he does not know what is in our hearts. Despite our losses and our weak condition, we will not surrender. And, surely, General Washington will lead us to victory!

Even so, it is difficult not to be discouraged. We know that we face a hard winter here. And the British are snug and warm in their beds in our captured capital of Philadelphia.

8

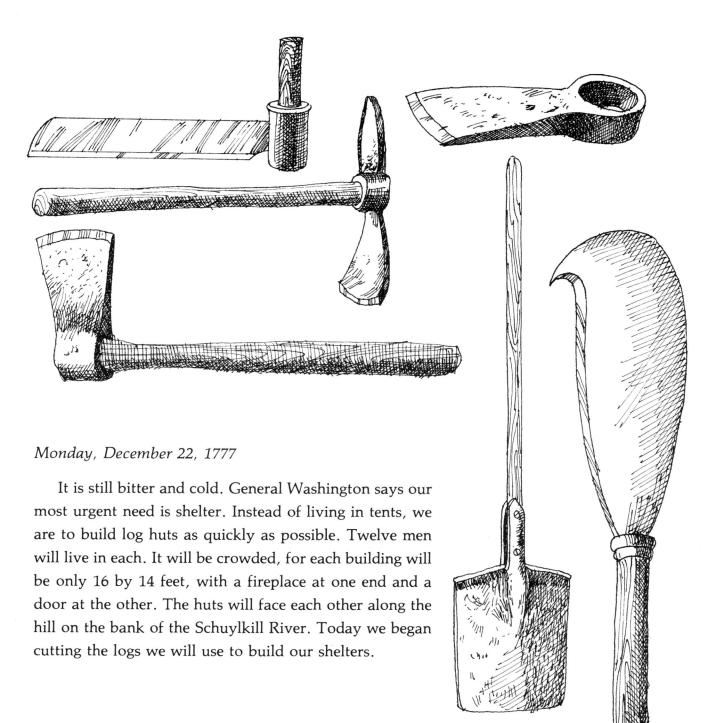

Monday, December 22, 1777

It is still bitter and cold. General Washington says our most urgent need is shelter. Instead of living in tents, we are to build log huts as quickly as possible. Twelve men will live in each. It will be crowded, for each building will be only 16 by 14 feet, with a fireplace at one end and a door at the other. The huts will face each other along the hill on the bank of the Schuylkill River. Today we began cutting the logs we will use to build our shelters.

9

We have been ordered to turn our tents in to the quartermaster as soon as the cabins are ready, but already the men grumble about this. The thought has occurred to all of us that our tents, thrown over the roofs, would help keep in some warmth. It promises to be a cruel winter, and the wind sweeping off the river chills us to the bone. I have already seen some of the men tearing the canvas tents into strips to wrap about their bodies, and especially their feet and legs. I fear the quartermaster will not get many tents back!

We have still received no uniforms. This army is indeed a strange-looking group—dressed in buckskin shirts, linsey-woolsey breeches, and blankets with holes cut in them for our heads to fit through. It is no wonder the British soldiers laugh at our raggle-taggle troops.

Still, they did not laugh at Trenton nor at Princeton. At these battles, General Washington rode ahead of the troops—encouraging us, and never fearing for his own life. And we drove the British back—in spite of their superior numbers!

Yesterday, several squads received issues of shoes, but we received none. And food has not yet arrived. The Continental Congress, which fled to York, Pennyslvania, when the British took Philadelphia, has determined the daily rations for each soldier. We are supposed to receive a pound and a half of flour or bread, a pound of meat or fish, or three-quarters of a pound of pork. But for the last four days, there has been no fresh meat at all, and only a few ounces of flour. From this we make "fire cake." We moisten the flour to make a thick paste, and then grill it over hot embers. It tastes terrible—but it is food.

Friday, December 26, 1777

The snow is now up to our ankles. More men fall sick every day, and their moans can be heard in the cold, dark night. It is hard to keep up our courage. Were it not for General Washington, we would surely lose heart. He endures the same conditions we suffer. What he can bear, we can bear, too. Surely, with such a leader, we cannot fail!

The General sends many messages seeking supplies—but still none come. There are more than 11,000 men here at Valley Forge—and at least 3,000 are not fit to march or fight.

Many local farmers refuse to provide us with food, for the British pay them more for it. Still, our Christmas dinner was better than we expected: a bit of fowl, cabbage, and turnips.

General Washington is concerned that our soldiers may become so desperate as to steal food, threatening the farmers hereabouts. He urges cooperation between the soldiers and citizens, but I fear there will be more trouble as the winter wears on. Already several men have been caught stealing food and supplies. They will be punished, but I cannot say I blame them much.

We are camped so near the British that a watch must be kept at all times. Many reports come in, both true and false, of enemy movements.

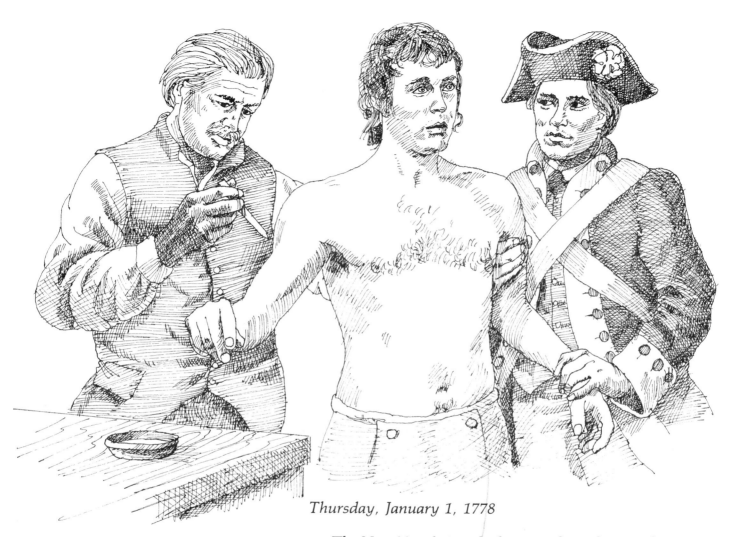

Thursday, January 1, 1778

The New Year brings little warmth or cheer with it. But at least our hut is finished. When we are not on duty, we huddle around the fire to keep warm. Each time a soldier goes in or out, we must stoke the fire again—and since we must use green wood, there is thick smoke all the time. But we are thankful for our shelter. Some of the men are still in tents, being too ill to work.

There is much typhus and smallpox in the camp, and the doctors are inoculating as many soldiers as possible every day. They have also given us sulfur to burn in our cabins. This is foul-smelling and adds to our misery—but the doctors say it will keep disease away. Yet more men become sick every day. Luckily, the soldiers in my squad suffer only from extreme cold and fatigue—so far.

General Washington announced that Congress has voted us one month's extra pay for our patience and loyalty to the cause of independence. We could only smile at this, for we have not received any pay since October.

When will supplies come? We still need clothing, particularly shoes and stockings. And because there is no soap to wash with, more than half of us suffer with lice. How will we last the winter?

Yesterday, one of our lads tried to desert. He was caught near Valley Creek, not far from General Washington's headquarters. He was given one hundred lashes.

Surgeon's Instruments

Lafayette

Sunday, January 4, 1778

The Schuylkill River is now frozen over.

Several foreign officers have joined us in our war against the British. Most popular is the Marquis de Lafayette, from France. He is a young man of nineteen or twenty. Count Pulaski, who came here from Poland to join the American Army, is another favorite. And Baron de Kalb is a German major-general much liked by the men.

We hear that a boat has been captured from the enemy at Wilmington. There are supposedly many supplies on board—flour, pork, arms, and clothing—perhaps even shoes! I pray that these provisions will reach us soon. But it is difficult to move supplies about the countryside. Citizens with wagons demand high payments for moving provisions. And many are as likely to smuggle goods to the British in Philadelphia as to bring them to the Continental Army.

More and more men are deserting. Many soldiers have been stealing food from citizens in the surrounding area.

Pulaski

De Kalb

Ammunition Carrier

Most of these soldiers are simply hungry, but some are stealing for a profit. General Washington says that those who plunder will be punished. Even so, he may soon have to order that provisions be seized from farmers.

Food is so scarce that yesterday we received no ration at all. Now a strange call is making the rounds of the camp: "No meat, no soldier!" Sometimes this cry is longer and sadder: "No meat, no flour, no coat, no soldier!"

I pity General Washington, who must hear these cries. He certainly knows that it is the sound of near-mutiny. As a corporal, I should stop the men in my hut from this unmilitary chanting. Instead, I join in it myself. I am as hungry and sad as they are. What are we ragged fools doing in this miserable place? How much longer can this army hold together? I begin to think of May—my enlistment is up then. Perhaps I shall leave the army and go home to Connecticut, where I belong.

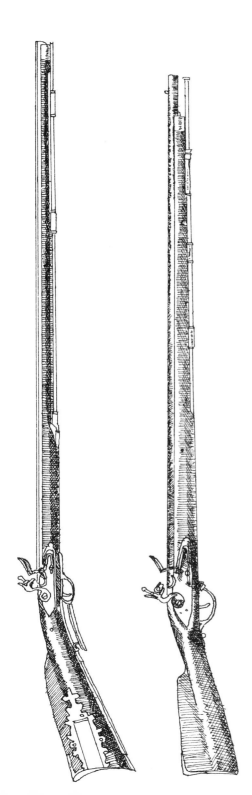

Rain has turned the campground into a muddy horror.

Yesterday, one of our officers and two soldiers were killed in a skirmish with the enemy.

The winter is hard on our poor horses. They stand thin and shivering out-of-doors and are fed practically nothing. It is pitiful to see. Many fall to the ground and freeze to death. We cannot bury them deeply, for the earth is frozen. The stench is sickening.

Our rifles are in poor condition, and we have little powder to fire them. If we were attacked right now, we would not have the strength to flee.

Still there are no shoes for most of the men. General Washington is trying to barter for leather, so that shoes can be made. But who would make them? And what have we to barter? Our situation grows more desperate every day.

General Howe has offered a sixteen-dollar prize to any Continental soldier who will desert and serve the Crown! I fear that many will go. Not I! In spite of our present difficulty, I still believe in our cause. But I miss my family and wish this terrible war were over...and the winter, as well.

When I am on duty as Corporal of the Guard, I see my ragged men at their posts, half frozen in slush and mud. Many of the soldiers stand on their hats to keep their bare feet off the snow. And some have had to have limbs amputated because they have been too long in the freezing temperatures.

Hundreds lie sick of typhus and smallpox in our hospital cabins. The doctors can do nothing for them.

The chanting has begun again tonight: "No bread, no soldier!" I think seriously of leaving the army in May—if I survive till then.

Tuesday, January 27, 1778

At last, some clothes have arrived. They came from Lancaster, where they were made by citizens sympathetic to our cause. Also, one hundred-fifty soldiers from Virginia arrived today. They were horrified when they saw our condition.

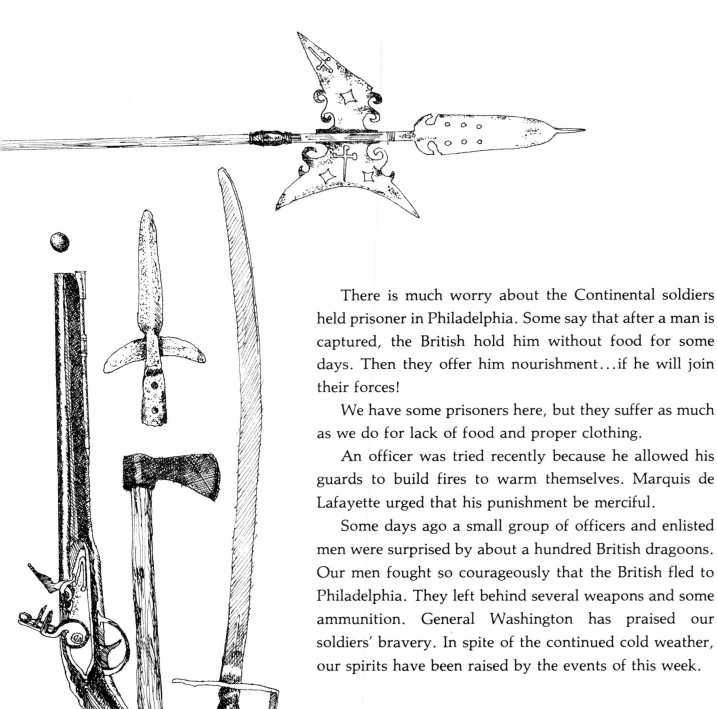

There is much worry about the Continental soldiers held prisoner in Philadelphia. Some say that after a man is captured, the British hold him without food for some days. Then they offer him nourishment...if he will join their forces!

We have some prisoners here, but they suffer as much as we do for lack of food and proper clothing.

An officer was tried recently because he allowed his guards to build fires to warm themselves. Marquis de Lafayette urged that his punishment be merciful.

Some days ago a small group of officers and enlisted men were surprised by about a hundred British dragoons. Our men fought so courageously that the British fled to Philadelphia. They left behind several weapons and some ammunition. General Washington has praised our soldiers' bravery. In spite of the continued cold weather, our spirits have been raised by the events of this week.

20

Saturday, February 7, 1778

Bad weather has returned after one or two almost pleasant days. Somehow, things seem worse when sleet and cold assault us. The men are sick and discouraged. General Washington tries valiantly to cheer us, but he is saddened by the hardships we must endure. He is also concerned that there are few re-enlistments. The Continental Army grows smaller every day—death, sickness, and desertion take their toll. We are starving. And we have not been paid for several months.

We hear that Mistress Washington is on her way to Valley Forge. I often think of my own wife and daughters. Will I ever see them again?

Friday, February 13, 1778

Mistress Washington arrived in camp last Tuesday, after some difficulty in crossing the Schuylkill. Already she has brought comfort to many. Each day, she visits the sick in their huts.

I am heartened that we continue to survive this ordeal.
But if only the spring would come.

We hear rumors that France will support us in our
struggle. Marquis de Lafayette assures us that this will
happen.

Wednesday, February 25, 1778

A miracle has happened! Yesterday several men suddenly observed the river come alive with fish! At first they thought it was chunks of floating ice they were seeing, for the recent thaw has loosened much ice. But it was hundreds upon hundreds of shad! I am told they rarely leave the Delaware River to swim all the way up the Schuylkill. Yet there they were—leaping and struggling in the low water of the river. Word spread quickly. Some of us beat the water to force the fish toward shore. Then others waded out and netted the fish. This mysterious run of shad has ended the winter's famine—for a time.

Friday, February 27, 1778

Freezing weather. The shad are still running in the river. We catch and salt down barrels of them for future use.

A foreign officer named Baron von Steuben arrived at camp a few days ago. It is said that he has been in the service of the Prussian king and comes to instruct us in marching and drilling. Heaven knows, we can use his experience in the military arts.

Von Steuben

Saturday, February 28, 1778

The Baron inspected us yesterday. His face betrayed his astonishment, when he saw the condition of our clothing and equipment. We are in rags. Our rifles are rusty, and many will not fire. But there is a hint of humor in the Baron's eyes. Somehow, I think he is up to the challenge of teaching us to drill properly. He has difficulty speaking English, so he communicates mostly in French. Colonel Alexander Hamilton, who speaks French, translates for him.

Sunday, March 1, 1778

General Washington confers daily with von Steuben, and I hear that this newcomer will be our inspector-general.

It is strange to think that thousands of us here have seen battle and yet know nothing of proper drilling

procedure. It will be good to march and move about with some purpose. Perhaps the exercise will give us warmth as well as skill!

Do I imagine it, or is there just a hint of spring in the air?

Saturday, March 7, 1778

The Baron has accomplished military wonders in these few short days. We are becoming a disciplined army. Often General Washington watches our maneuvers and smiles with approval.

Rumors abound. We hear that the French will help our cause; that five hundred cattle are expected daily; that the British will attack any day. No matter—we begin to feel ready for anything! Our spies in Philadelphia tell us the British troops are restless and that General Howe has resigned. But still, the Redcoats have not attacked.

Tuesday, March 10, 1778

At last, some supplies are coming in...but we are still in need of more men. Many have died during the terrible winter.

Oh, how my poor back aches from bayonet drill! Before the Baron came, all we used our bayonets for was to roast pieces of salt pork over a fire.

Sunday, March 15, 1778

At last! Grass begins to appear, and we have seen robins. We hear frogs croaking at the river's edge. General Washington has issued orders that the camp be thoroughly cleaned. There is a feeling of hope among the men.

Monday, March 23, 1778

For several days now, almost the entire army has gathered around the drill field to watch Baron von Steuben drill the model company. Hour after hour, he shouts out his commands in a curious mixture of English, German, and French.

28

Often he forgets the English command—and gives a new one that mixes everyone up. But he does not seem to mind it when everyone is amused by this. Indeed, he seems to realize that laughter is good for us!

We have shifted the squads about so that both new and experienced men drill together. The recruits learn from the old campaigners. Four new men have joined my squad, and I drill them daily in the new commands.

Yesterday, I heard that shoes were available. Those men who needed them were told to report to the supply hut. But I was on duty as Corporal of the Guard. When my shift ended I immediately went there, but every pair of shoes was gone.

Wednesday, April 8, 1778

The camp seems a new place. The men play practical jokes on one another, and we cannot help but laugh. We are under strict orders to be neat and clean and freshly shaved. Even though we are not splendidly dressed, at least most of us are *dressed!* We have finally received stockings, caps, buckles... and even combs.